God Damned Avalon

Critical Acclaim

Brandon Pitts,
Poet, author of *Tender in the Age of Fury* and *In the Company of Crows*:

> "Paul Edward Costa writes towards the future, his creativity acting as a barometer to coming trends. *God Dammed Avalon* serves as a testament to his command of Flash Fiction and his comfort in the radically changing medium of written words."

Michelle Hillyard,
Poet and Board Member of the Mississauga Writers' Group:

> "Paul's collection demonstrates his unique ability to couple the fantastical with the concrete, creating dreamlike (yet realistic) worlds for the reader to explore while pondering the great questions of life, love, and death."

Laurence Hutchman,
Poet and Former Professor:

> "Paul Edward Costa's *God Damned Avalon* is an exciting collection of flash fiction. Through unusual plots, weird characters, and unexpected shifts, he creates a surreal atmosphere rearranging our concept of time and space"

Efetobore Mike-Ifeta,
Poet and Organizer, Host of The Talent Next Door and the MAKE Open Mic:

> "Using paradox, imagery, and symbolism, Paul Edward Costa invites us into what may seem otherworldly at first, but the universe that he so cleverly conjures up in *God Damned Avalon* couldn't be any closer to the human condition and our unrelenting fate as earthlings. The duality of beauty and pain, of life and death, of hope and despair, is hidden rather masterfully in the stories of *God Damned Avalon*."

God Damned Avalon

Flash Fiction

Paul Edward Costa

Library and Archives Canada Cataloguing in Publication

Title: God damned Avalon: Flash Fiction by Paul Edward Costa.

Names: Costa, Paul Edward, 1989- author.

Description: Includes bibliographical references and index.

Identifiers: Canadiana (print) 20200378120
Canadiana (ebook) 20200378155

ISBN 9781771615327 (softcover) ISBN 9781771615334 (PDF)
ISBN 9781771615341 (EPUB) ISBN 9781771615358 (Kindle)

Subjects: Ukrainians—Québec   (Province)—Val-d'Or—History—20th
century. | LCSH: Ukrainians—Québec (Province)—Val-d'Or—
Social conditions—20th century. | LCSH: Ukrainians—Québec
(Province)—Val-d'Or—Social life and customs—20th century. |
LCSH: Val-d'Or (Québec)—History—20th century. | LCSH: Val-
d'Or (Québec)—Social conditions—20th century. | LCSH: Val-
d'Or (Québec)—Social life and customs—20th century.

Classification: LCC PS8605.O872726 G63 2020
DDC C813/.6—dc23

Published by Mosaic Press, Oakville, Ontario, Canada, 2020.
www.mosaic-press.com

Cover Design by Rahim Piracha

ONTARIO ARTS COUNCIL
CONSEIL DES ARTS DE L'ONTARIO
an Ontario government agency
un organisme du gouvernement de l'Ontario

We acknowledge the Ontario Arts Council for their
support of our publishing program
Ontario Creates

Funded by the Government of Canada
Financé par le gouvernement du Canada | Canada

MOSAIC PRESS
1252 Speers Road, Units 1 & 2
Oakville, Ontario L6L 5N9
phone: (905) 825-2130

www.mosaic-press.com info@mosaic-press.com

Dedication

This book is dedicated to Brandon Pitts. Thank you for all the support, encouragement, and camaraderie you've shown me.

Biographic Note

Photo taken by Michelle Hillyard

Paul Edward Costa is a writer, spoken word artist, teacher, and the 2019-2021 Poet Laureate for the City of Mississauga. He has featured at many poetry reading series in the Greater Toronto Area and has published over 60 poems and stories in literary journals such as Bewildering Stories, Lucent Dreaming Magazine, Auroras and Blossoms Poetry Journal, and The Gyroscope Review. His first full length book of poetry "The Long Train of Chaos" was published by Kung Fu Treachery Press. He also curates/hosts the YTGA Open Mic Series, the Outer Haven

Poetry Series, and won the Mississauga Arts Council's 2019 MARTY Award for Emerging Literary Arts.

Facebook: https://m.facebook.com/PaulEdwardCosta/
YouTube: https://www.youtube.com/PaulEdwardCosta
Instagram: https://www.instagram.com/paul.edward.costa/
Twitter: @paul_e_costa

Statement by the Author

I started writing poetry as a teenager. This interest expanded into fiction soon after I turned twenty (but I still kept writing poems). As such, this book shows an interesting point in my development. The surrealism or experimentalism of these pieces comes from the fact that I still had a lot of poetic ideas involving atmosphere and imagery in my head when I wrote them. The challenge became fusing these inspirations with levels of plot and narrative to make them engaging for a reader. My love of genre fiction helped that goal. It gave rise to many of the horror, thriller, fantasy, or science fiction parts of this book. I aimed to arrange the pieces in a way that flowed logically through an abstract journey with recurring symbols and tropes. However, that journey may not be the same for you as it is for me. The beauty of abstraction (in appropriate doses) is its ability to make art become a mirror of discovery for the reader, in which a variety of people are able to project their unique experiences into the work. This can bring readers to an external reflection of their inner selves. It can indirectly lead to realizations they wouldn't have been able to previously approach head-on. I hope these stories offer some insight, as well as entertainment, as they explore a range of worlds, ideas, and characters.

Table of Contents

The following stories in this collection were previously published, in full or in part, in the following periodicals, whose editors the author thanks:

"Distorted Reflections of a Pilgrim" previously published in Queen Mob's Tea House

"A Sailboat on the Radio Waves" previously published in Emerge Literary Journal Issue #9

"Patience and Disassociation" previously published in The Bookends Review

"The Silent Minority" previously published in Literary Orphans

"A Ghost's Guide to Scorched Elm Drive" previously published in Enduring Puberty Press

"Garden Laundry Candle" previously published in Yesteryear Fiction

"Green Martyrdom" previously published in Thrice Fiction Magazine #11

"The Forest Sprite Cannot Hear the Whispering Trees" previously published in Tiny Flames Press

"Chess Variants" previously published in Murmurs of Words

"The Lucid Dream of an Analog Clock" previously published in Peacock Journal

"Room Limit (I-IV)" previously published in Enduring Puberty Press

"The Zero Second" previously published in Yesteryear Fiction

"Tales of Telyhurst Castle: Gorgon Hall" previously published in Alien Mouth

"Tales of Telyhurst Castle: Reverent Arturo's Flock" previously published in Sein Und Werden

"The Widening Maw" previously published on The905: Contemporary Arts and Culture in the Region of Peel

"The Sad Masquerade" previously published in Mannequin Haus: A Journal of Literary Art

"Rainbows and Black Tumours" previously published in Lucent Dreaming Issue #4

"The Lone and Level Sands Will Stretch Far Away" previously published in Peacock Journal

"The Modern Theseus" previously published in Synaeresis: Arts + Poetry from Harmonia Press

Portions of "The Chronicle of Everything" previously published in Timber Journal

GOD DAMNED AVALON

Flash Fiction

PAUL EDWARD COSTA

Distorted Reflections of a Pilgrim

I don't know my beginning. I became aware of myself inside a cabin with two men and an old spherical astrolabe, which they promised would one day produce fire in the mound of kindling they'd piled beneath it. The men had black beards, long hair, plaid shirts, and suspenders. They ate strips of raw, salted fish as they sat cross-legged around the astrolabe's cluster of bronze rings. They stared at the sticks, twigs, and leaves they'd placed below it.

They promised a fire flashing white, green, blue, yellow, and crimson like no other source of light I'd seen. They complimented me on how still I was, and I sat waiting for longer then I felt I'd actually been there, until I realized that the fire wouldn't come,

1

"Yes…but that storm only strikes those who leave," he said. I saw him land a hook on the statue's side. "Anyone getting close right now is still following a field of blooming tulips."

I shook my head with my eyes shut tight.

"That means you'll freeze if you go out there," I said.

"Now you're using your noggin," said the man. He ducked and weaved through imagined jabs. "I'll freeze, as will you, and anyone else who goes out after they've come in."

"I can't go back," I said, and the man said nothing. He let me absorb the thought I'd spoken out loud. I walked to the statue on the pedestal and told the man how I'd gotten there.

"I hate to be the one to tell you, but you'll realize all the rest have too, finding themselves in that cabin, guarded by the two men, before seeing through their facades, and coming to this… *institute* for some real answers," the man stopped boxing with the statue as he leaned on his knees. He let out a wheezing laugh. The breath he exhaled came out as steam from under his hood.

"Are there answers here?" I said.

"In a way," said the man.

I said "How do I find them? What do I need?"

"You need the kind of masochism that horrifies the faithful," he said.

He went back to sparring with the statue.

I thought of the traumatized deacons I'd met as they fled the museum.

I thought of the two men in the cabin who stared at kindling under the spherical astrolabe.

As I did, I looked past the man and the statue he fought to the large, Birchwood double doors behind which lay further branches of the museum. The black ink on them showed a huge multitude of tiny, intricately drawn figures moving towards—and falling over—a downwards curve of the line on which they stood, with the whole piece becoming an increasingly blotchy splatter of blobs as my eye moved down.

"What will I find past there? Where's the end?" I said.

"It's hard to say—I grabbed the first spot," he said, "but I've heard of a room with a monk who gives in to temporary insanity, smashes the furniture, and attacks all who are still inside with the broken leg of a wooden table; of course, he finds it very rude if you confronts him about his violence when he's calm...others have talked about places where people lie on their fronts while allowing their night terrors to squat on their backs and suck patches of skin between their shoulder blades into purple blemishes...I know there's a hall somewhere filled with painful—but not fatal—gases, where you can only escape by following the instructions of a guide whose gas mask muffles their words...word has also gotten around of a torture room where each session finishes with the victim writing an apology to their torturer, using their own blood, because working the machines that administer such suffering is hard on the wrists of the operator, apparently." The man looked down at his own bloodied, broken, and swollen hands. "But they'll find no sympathy from me." He chuckled and continued boxing with the statue. "In addition..." he started saying.

"No," I said. "Stop. My palms just get getting clammier whenever you tell me...but, I know I can't go back...I need to see these places, don't I?"

The man nodded.

"What now?" I said.

"You go and find your pain," said the man boxing on the pedestal with the marble statue.

Before I went to do so I looked at his disfigured hands. I turned and walked back to the abandoned ticket counter. I rummaged through its drawers until I found a thick roll of tape. I taped my hands and wrists to keep the bones inside set and to pad my knuckles. I walked back to the double doors.

My mouth opened and I looked down. After a moment, I looked up, closed my jaw and shut my eyes. I shook my head as I placed my hands on the handles of the Birchwood doors, opened them, and entered the rest of the museum

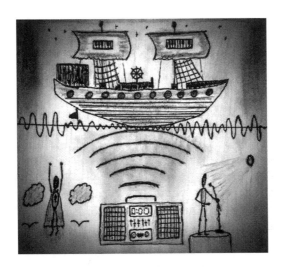

Sailboat on the Radio Waves

As a child I always had to go to bed at nine o'clock, although I usually fell asleep much later. At nine o'clock I'd go into my room and crawl into bed. My father turned off the lights. Sometimes I still lay awake in the darkness of my room when my parents went to bed and shut off the hallway light. I felt truly alone and at the mercy of the night in those moments, lost in a small boat and helpless before a force or feeling I could barely comprehend. I listened to the radio set at a soft volume. I heard songs of the daytime, pop music I remembered from the grocery store or from the car after school. Those sounds reminded me of day. They made me feel glad.

Usually I feel asleep at this point. But my dark mother Insomnia sometimes led me further into the vast unexplored lands past the gates of midnight. It felt like I alone occupied an outpost all alone in a black land filled with twilight versions of the places I knew well from the day. On these nights, when my consciousness ventured past midnight, I heard stranger and stranger messages on the radio. I found myself in small comedy clubs whose wisdom I couldn't understand...

...it always makes me laugh when a day gets totally wasted and someone says something to try and cheer you up like "oh, there's always tomorrow," or "you can make up for this weekend next weekend" (mild laughter). Isn't that just the stupidest thing? I mean, you just want to scream, "I only have a finite amount of time on this earth you know! There isn't any more! Once a day is gone, it's gone, and it isn't coming back!" (nervous laughter). If you do tomorrow what you were prevented from doing today, then you're just cutting into what tomorrow could have been (scattered laughs), and then you're only playing endless catch up. You wouldn't say to a kid who's dropped his ice cream, "oh, you can always get another," because if the first one hadn't fallen, he could have had two! (laughter and applause).

Afterwards I stumbled into the 1940's and heard the radio adventures of Superman, and I lost hold of my young self in the shifting shadows of my room...

...Faster than a speeding bullet...
More powerful than a locomotive...
Able to leap tall buildings in a single bound...
Look up in the sky! It's a bird! It's a plane!
It's Superman!
(Organ theme)

Today we begin a brand new story, the story of a menace which will lead Superman and his friends through many dangerous adventures...

Only the green digital clock on my nightstand held my journey to a linear path. Finally. after the crackling voices of the 1940's faded and I lay beneath the sheets with my eyes closed,

I always walked into a jazz club at the end of the night with dim pot lights hanging low from the ceiling, brick walls, and mysterious people huddled around small tables. I found myself in the strange court of a nocturnal kingdom deep in some downtown city past the quiet suburb where I lived. On the rare nights when I made it to this place the band on the smoky stage always played the same song. Brush sticks circled and massaged the snare drum, the upright bass walked like a lurching black cat, a forlorn muted trumpet murmured and cried, and a wise cool woman wearing a red dress crooned into her silver microphone, behind the smoke of the lit cigarette she held with poise and sophistication. The night spoke to me. It carried me off to sleep at last and enabled my dreams.

When I got older I could stay up as late as I wanted, go out with friends after sunset, or visit the fabled core of downtown, but I never wandered into the heart of the night like I did as a boy. I became a man and never found the mystic jazz club of my young, wakeful dreaming.

Patience and Disassociation

Cole Santos sat cross legged on his bed and tore open the letter for which he'd been waiting. In the weeks before its arrival he woke up early with a pounding heart, felt sweat in his palms whenever he checked the mailbox, and allowed himself to entertain fantasies about its possibly positive contents.

Cole read the letter.

He folded it neatly, inserted it back into its envelope, and gently placed the letter on the bedspread in front of him. He felt something move inside him. Cole inhaled and expanded his chest. He exhaled and collapsed it. He felt stillness within him once more. Cole raised one hand and looked at it. He clenched it into a

9

fist before relaxing it and opening his palm. He repeated this several times. Cole placed both hands on his knees when he'd finished.

A familiar and chilling tingle spread through Cole's body. It brought out mild goose bumps on his arms. It slackened his muscles. His mind thought about moving for a long time but his body remained perfectly still. He worried about this feeling after the first time it crept into him, but now it felt like the embrace of an old friend. The feeling's reliability silenced any internal conflict he had about its negative qualities. The feeling was not one of nothing itself. It felt like it was the only thing that comforted Cole when all else retreated and left him alone in black seas of infinite. He welcomed its presence as it inhabited him and shut down his senses, the senses which burned with rising passion and searing pain in alternating order when left to Cole's control.

Cole's eyelids began hanging heavily over the tops of his eyes. His lips rested together and his mouth didn't move as his nerves froze. His pupils darted around his surroundings, looking indirectly at the frayed fabric where the carpet met the wall, at the top of a distant building through the window and at the digital clock's still numbers in the eternity it took for a minute to pass. At last they looked up, half at the monotone, gray plaster ceiling above and half into his own skull. He blinked slowly and stared straight ahead, his detached gaze looking through everything in front of him. Cole's face reassumed the same catatonic stare he'd worn while motionless and seated behind his office's desk at 4:15pm on a Wednesday, that he'd worn while in the wicker basket of a hot air balloon three thousand feet above the Arizona desert, and that he'd worn while walking past the scene of a minutes old shooting on the streets of San Francisco's tenderloin district.

Thoughts began and died away half-finished in his head.

What if I waited for...
Maybe if I just...
Is it because...
Why does it always...

Cole remembered someone telling him once that all the strung together moments of absence, pain, and isolation in life would one day dissolve and become validated by the arrival of a golden, majestic reality, indescribable because no one had yet received it, but which could, and indeed would arrive any day now, as long as time continued marching forward.

Cole felt the need to lie down under his blankets and appropriate the darkness beneath them. The chill within him blossomed into a winter's fog that surrounded Cole, terraforming the space around him into a frigid and anesthetized eternity, a room of his own which he'd been to before and that he'd come back to again.

The Silent Minority

The sandwich didn't look like much at first.

The hands which held it belonged to a man sitting near me on the bus. I sat at the back, facing forward. He sat in front of me in a seat turned perpendicular to mine so that I had a side profile view of his form.

He had a young face, medium length blonde hair, a baseball t-shirt with sleeves coloured orange and the torso white, and a simple pair of blue jeans.

I felt like I'd seen him once before, reading quietly on a green field one sunny day, wearing the same clothes, but I hated him; I cannot remember why, and I struggled even then to articulate my distaste logically to a friend.

He leaned forward with his elbows resting on his knees. His feet pressed flat against the floor.

He held the sandwich in his left hand as he sat this way. I didn't see him take it out and I didn't know if he'd already been eating it when he got on the bus and sat down. One triangle-cut half had already been eaten and digested; the other half poked a quarter of the way out of a plastic zip-lock bag. It consisted of pale cold cuts pressed between two slices of whole wheat bread cleanly spread with mustard.

All this appeared generally normal, except that he showed signs of profound pain and discomfort while he ate the sandwich.

I hesitate to call it "his" because if he'd made it entirely on his own, and the desire to eat it was fully his, I imagine that he'd show some joy or satisfaction as he ate. It appeared instead that eating the sandwich was a matter in which he did not have the final say.

He chewed slowly, with his mouth closed and stretched down into a contemptuous frown.

Sometimes his hard eyes stared out at the world blurring by the window, at bare trees with clusters of rusted branches, endless powerlines, huge 1980's home satellites dishes, and monolithic brown apartments spaced far apart from each other as their stark geometric lines stood against the formless, gray sky. Sometimes he looked down and to the side at the sticky black floor of the bus with a collage of transfers and candy wrappers pressed onto its surface.

He swallowed the bite in his mouth. He closed his eyes and shook his head. A shiver snaked through his body. He stared straight ahead at nothing in particular, set his mouth into a frown, hesitated, raised the sandwich to his face, hesitated again, and tore a bite out of it with his teeth. He lowered the remaining sandwich without looking at it, resting his left arm on his knee again.

He chewed slowly, with his mouth closed and stretched down into a contemptuous frown.

He rolled his eyes up and muttered incoherently under his breath. I saw quick glimpses of the mutilated sandwich rolling around inside his mouth in its moist, massacred, and shapeless form. He exhaled heavily. His eyelids dropped apathetically over the top halves of his eyes as he swallowed again.

I never spoke with him because I felt completely unsure of how a man so singularly dedicated to a task such as his might react—he might offer either an epiphany, or confirm that epiphanies have long since abandoned this place.

On that afternoon I began asking myself *"What sort of malevolent force compels his continued consumption of the sandwich?"* before recognizing that force, with a start, as the same one driving me towards my own destination, or lack thereof.

Somehow I knew he would take another bite, but I made no effort to stop him, because I'm a firm believer in individual liberty. Ever since I once met a recovered addict who maintained his sobriety by listening to endless conspiracy theories on internet radio I've accepted that the best way to get on with things is to hurl oneself fanatically at a cause, any cause, because on contact I firmly believe we'll find that their surfaces—which we assumed were carved from noble granite—are actually made from an inflated nylon that will bounce us back as we accept the arrival of our sacrificial death by high velocity impact, and that we'll wake up shocked, slightly humbled, and capable of nothing but a dry laughter, without which we would only hear a silence echoing with our amplified faults.

And so I realized that he'll continue eating his sandwiches of compressed suffering just as I continue blindly traversing the remote city limits on public transit with no clear destination but an escape from the present moment.

I hope I'll see him again sometime, and maybe I'll even take the chance of speaking with him, when I'm certain that I'm traveling during the darkest night, on a bus bathed in the loneliest blue light, on a regional road running through the furthest industrial fields, in the all-consuming nightmare of wakefulness while the city dreams in its deepest sleep, at the lowest point of my own journey…then I'll reach out and speak with him, and maybe even make a connection, once I finally feel objective, undeniable despair reach up out of infinite and touch my shoulder.

A Ghost's Guide to Scorched Elm Drive

I turned onto Scorched Elm Drive. Bare trees lined the rain-damp streets. Their branches hung low like fleshless fingers. It felt like they beckoned me further along the road. The whole street was like an esophagus forcing along its length. I stepped over garbage and flat cigarette butts on the ground.

I walked to the townhouse where my friend Zade held an autumn gathering of a few neighborhood friends. We sat in a circle in her basement and linked hands. She'd lit candles with wax shaped into stacks of ancient Persian pillows as we drifted through a collective meditation. She kept an analog tape recorder going during our silent session. We listened to the playback.

A ghost of our street began speaking through the crackling static. This is what it said.

***

Midnight may be the dead hour, and 3:00am the witching hour, but 10:00am is the horror of a dead night resurrected and stumbling down abandoned side streets without traffic.

The daytime fog enveloping the streets is the same overcast sky in every old sepia photo of this neighborhood. That fog set in slowly over generations until children grew up blind as the elderly drew their curtains closed and took refuge in the crinkled images of their memories. These were, to them, distant kingdoms of vibrant colour where the blind stayed out of sight and out of mind.

We ghosts can see what you feel. I look down and see filthy water gurgling along the gutters as it carries dozens of rose-tinted contact lenses into the sewers.

Have you seen the old man walking along the sidewalk wearing shoes wrapped thoroughly with black electrical tape? He is of much wisdom. If you give him a nod he'll smile and says "this isn't 2020; I'm still dreaming of 1981," before tapping his forehead and walking off.

You may not know that a man nearby makes crayon drawings of children being eaten by wolves.

We ghosts can only huff and puff against the brown and gray walls of eternal brick.

Our ethereal fists leave what looks like water stains on the sides of the apartments and strip malls, so I developed a way to speak into people's thoughts after giving up on the urge to physically intervene with my immaterial body.

***

Myself, Zade, and the other guests spoke due to pure gut instinct.

"What do you say to them?" each member of the circle asked.

After a fuzzy burst of white noise, the ghost continued speaking, though we could not tell if this was a response or simply the next part of its speech.

***

I met a trembling woman washing dishes nearby using soap from a dispenser painted with faded tulips against a dull pink background. She stood in front of a window overlooking the spiders on her crumbling balcony. She wore an-off white pull-over sweater with cracked kitten designs on its front. I've occupied this street long enough to know her sweater was one like a girls with perms wear in a class pictures from the 1980s on walls of the local school.

She asked me *"Which magical beast tore open our black garbage bags and spread their contents through the grass on the boulevards? It scattered used tissues, coffee lids crushed flat, and cheap flyers everywhere. Did their positions on the lawn match some mysterious constellation?"*

I told her it was simply the mess of a hungry raccoon.

She said *"But I thought I heard an old 1800s ghost locomotive's steam whistle puff through last night, while angels beat their wings over my roof."*

I told her "You heard a commuter train…and the soft patter beating over your roof was only the rain."

***

The tape returned to incoherent static when Zade released her grip on the hands of the guests to her left and right. She fell over onto her side. She lay on the carpet while shivering, blinking rapidly, and moving her lips without speaking.

Garden Laundry Candle

Somewhere a cluster of linens lie on the grass, layered into the shape of a pyramid. A single scented candle rests on the peak of this soft structure. Its wick burns like magnesium, sending out

19

a glow to places whose illumination is counterbalanced only by areas with an extreme absence of light…

***

The sad stone children smeared with dirt ask that you remain silent. They each hold one finger to their granite lips.

Enjoy this moment of peace and reflection. Don't look at it as the present. Don't look at is as now. If you do, you may forget and devalue everything within arm's reach. Imagine this close cluster of time as the past with yourself standing in the white light of the future looking back in sorrow.

And why not sorrow? This garden hold's dusk's mystical light like a crystal. The dark grass murmurs with an internal mystery. And the classical white youthful statues! They insist upon your silence. Some gaze around in wonder. They hold still and withhold information. They suggest the nearby presence of terrible, beautiful wonders. You don't feel scared or bored. Curiosity remains, prevailing in the blessed absence of heavy stones like satisfaction or fear. Such pure feelings in this dreamlike place.

But of course you look back at this scene with sorrow while in the future's white light. Now cease your dark regretful imaginings. Open your eyes. You are not looking back at this serenity from a blind empty future. You are standing in the now, and now is this midnight garden of awe, and this realization is a gift.

A holy ache courses through your muscles. You sit on the garden's wrought iron bench. You feel spent and content. No paths presently lead out of the garden, but you now feel able to forge one someday with confidence. What is this feeling? A sense of accomplishment overcomes your mind. What did you achieve? What did you construct?

A white tower rises far away in the night fog behind you. It lies in another isolated place within these black lands of midnight. Blood stains its stucco walls. Sounds of life and laughter echo from its top rooms. Green neon letters spell W E L C O M E over the tower's arched front door. The first three letters are burned out. Spotlights shine through midnight's fog from the tower's roof. These lights don't reach the garden where you sit. You never turn around in order to meet their gaze with yours.

What does reach you are innumerable groans from the tower's base and from deep beneath its foundations. They still come out of the dark past to claw at your ears.

What's that in your hands, hanging limply between your knees? You still hold the antique crossbow made of brass and wood from a yew tree because the groans never come alone. They bring their living hosts: ravenous skeletons, half crushed and caked with dirt, pulling themselves through the dark with bony fingers, leaving drag marks rippling through the blackness. One with a bolt through its skull remains mangled in the garden's closed gate behind you, the same gate you used when entering this place. Its one frail arm lies stretched out on the grass with a single index finger pointing towards you, followed by its skeletal face, whose bone brow and open jaw twist into an expression of rage, silently screaming a grave accusation in your direction.

It feels like the only thing left to do is sit quietly on the garden's bench while surveying what lies ahead with introspective contemplation. Don't move your body. Become like the sad stone children, except for your eyes. Let them drift to the right and to the left in their sockets. Feel them move in your skull, soft spherical organs unchanged since yours birth. Feel them move while surveying the tight, tall expansive hedge marking the farthest edge of the garden. Vines and branches twist in on themselves towards a singularity. Green leaves cover them in clusters so close only a few streams of wind pass in from the night beyond. The hedge's structural complexities bend, guide and morph the wind into whispers snaking through the garden. Sitting still, almost frozen, you listen hard to the whispers balanced maddeningly between music and language.

The sad stone children smeared with dirt ask that you remain silent. They each hold one finger to their granite lips.

WELCOME

Green Martyrdom

Do you remember the day you travelled to the island?
 I don't remember the day I travelled to the island.
 I dress in my black suit and go there instead.
 I don't go there.
 I go to the island's broken foggy remnants.
 I don't move.
 I wander into the impressions left on my mind by little rivers.
They travelled across the grasslands covering the island. Each tiny
stream grew fatter until the web became a low flood soaking the
ground. Why? Water fell viciously from the sky. It washed over
my face. *Is this rain?* Dainty fairy droplets didn't fall. Fat blobbed

23

aquatic bombs crashed down on everything in a constant wave. In my black suit I stood again on the long dock. My cerebral boat disappeared into the mist. I adjusted the sniper rifle slung across my back and ventured inland.

I walked along the coastal road. First, a row of sixteen houses lay before the rolling green hills. Fifteen stood there, quaintly run down. The sixteenth existed only as a black skeletal frame burned hollow. I went inside to investigate. No signs indicated they set fire to the house anticipating my arrival. Moss grew from the ash inside. A pale shirtless young man in beige pants sat at a wooden table with a manual typewriter on it. A nude young Celtic woman came in, wrapped her arms around him from behind and kissed his cheek. She left him to his work. They paid me no attention. I looked at the page in his typewriter. Its first sentence read:

"I wander into the impressions left on my mind by little rivers..."

Who would write such fanciful delusions? I strangled him with my garrote write. He kicked over the table and went still. The girl lay naked on a mound of hay in the corner. She slept on her back. She held a spread out impressionistic pose. Her long waves of red hair mixed with the straw. My vision blurred when I placed my hands over her mouth. I kept them there until her soft breathing stopped. For some reason my face felt wet again. I wiped my eyes and the confusion went away. I left the ruined house.

I saw waist-high walls crisscrossing the hilly landscape ahead of me. They divided the fields of long abandoned farms into geometric shapes. Green hills in front of me slowly ascended into the low gray sky.

My priest rode up in his dark rusted tractor. He once baptized my head in a broken stone chapel with some clear liquid I can't describe. I knew him, though I couldn't remember the exact location of our last meeting. I got in the cart hitched up behind his tractor. I sat cross legged. We puttered off through the hills. He turned around and yelled to me over the sounds of his the engine:

"I just came from that heathen's house. He wouldn't even *pretend* to pray at his dying mother's bedside..." he pursed his lips and angrily shook his head.

I stared at him while he spoke.

We stopped at a ridge overlooking some ruins. I got out of the tractor's cart and stood at the edge. My priest stayed at the wheel. He sighed and looked off through the sheets of water falling from the gray sky. I dug the stock of my rifle into the soft grassy ground, held the barrel and leaned on it while I looked down. My eyes wandered. A roofless chapel stood with half a cross over its doorway and weeds growing out of every crack. Other structures lay around it. What else? How about a hill covered with a ring of trees? *Yes, that sounds good. The soft curves of the hill make me feel free.* Next to that hill rested the foundations of a rectangular building.

"What's that?" I ask out loud rhetorically.

My priest answered "The old guard slept there."

"Yes, barracks," I said in response. I liked the sound of that. I liked the rigidity of those foundations.

A circular crater sunk into the ground at the edge of the village. It looked too big for cooking. It also didn't match the shape of any other building, so it couldn't be an empty foundation. Anything could have been there. Anything could be there still.

A sudden wave of nausea and vague illness passed over me. I felt woozy. Then my eyes glazed over. I found myself thinking: *is this all there is?* The broken work of stonemasons stretched off in every direction. Between it grew even green grass. I hunched over the rifle and held it like a cane. Every one of my joints stiffened. I felt old. I imagined a small monster with a thick beard grinning from ear to ear amidst the ruins. Its eyes remained fixed on me no matter what it did. It walked into the church, skipping for no reason. After that it stormed out muttering over its shoulder. It approached the tree crowned hill with wide eyes and both its arms outstretched. Once inside the trees, the little monster scrunched its face and shook with concentration until its soft face gained permanent lines. It wandered off in a daze over the hill ignoring all the blobs of water falling from above. It started walking in routines around the old barracks. It stamped out flowers underfoot. At that moment I found myself projecting an intense hatred onto the little creature. Still, I couldn't imagine how it might end up at the empty crater but I hoped it would get there and find a way to construct something in the void.

When I looked up I saw the far coast rising gradually into a seaside cliff. A Celtic stone castle stood on that risen edge. My joints loosened. I un-slung my rifle and moved forewords. I remembered my mission. Or I decided what to do. I wasn't sure which.

I jogged uphill to the castle. My feet pounded over rocky patches growing out of the grass. I felt amazed that my boots held together. I moved through the droplets of water beating down from the sky and washing down the hill. I slowed down at the top, took the sniper rifle off safety, and looked around. No one remained in the fragments of this old castle. I couldn't be too careful. It was two thousand years since this civilization fell. I crept under shaky stone archways, around lonely sections of wall, and through roofless chambers.

Finally I ended up at an empty window right on the edge of land. It looked over a sheer cliff out at the raging ocean beyond. I leaned out. In the tall cliff underneath me lay a massive black cavern. Coastal waters stormed and blew into it. A great hollowness occupied the ground beneath my feet. A gentle chill touched my spine. Ahead lay a vast ocean until the horizon. Waves crashed all over its murky surface. They looked like the palpitations of something below. I couldn't see land across it but I knew my home sat thousands of kilometers over the water. The edge of this island represented the closest I could ever get to it. I put the bi-pod of my sniper rifle on the empty window sill and gazed through its powerful scope.

Across the ocean I saw a version of myself wearing a gray suit in my house's garden. My gray clad self sat at a laptop on an iron table over there. I scanned that garden through my rifle's scope from this seaside castle, looking for approaching demons. They might arrive shortly to attack my gray-suited self. My mind's eye pictured an image of the demons quietly surrounding my oblivious self in the yard. Now I know why I came to the edge of this wet green island with my weapon. I waited for the demons to approach my home across the ocean. I zoomed the lens in on the laptop my gray clad self sat at thousands of kilometers away. The first sentence on that screen read

"Do you remember the day you travelled to the island?"

I looked up from the rifle, saw the blank horizon past the ocean, then looked back through the sniper scope. I saw my gray-suited self alone in the garden filled with nightshade and stone angels, working at a laptop on the wrought iron table. I held my weapon's grip and thought for longer than could have been necessary. Sight and awareness connected me to him across the ocean but I never felt so alone. I fired. *This must be rain I feel on my face.* Every set stone and leafy plant both on this island and in the garden shifted slightly as the shot cracked across the hills and echoed over the ocean.

Heads Filled with False Imaginings

The mountain pass overlooked a climate of ever present dusk above the forest of colossal pine trees. Their spores of black fungi spewed green mist above the treeline. No one ventured into those woods and fewer could conceive of an experience beneath the folds of their dark branches. The smell coming from the forest made nostrils as far off as the mountain pass recoil at the rank stench of vegetative decay.

The knights whose crusade it was to abduct travelers here waited behind the bushes without stealth or subtlety. They wore old chainmail and white tunics emblazoned with the floral ink pattern of their order. They wore metal cowl helmets and had no skin on the lower halves of their faces. There they showed a permanent grin of tendons and teeth. Without lips, their saliva glands pumped out drool without restriction or restraint. They clung to halberds taller than themselves.

They kept only one goal in their minds: abduct travelers from this road running through the twisted forest of a long broken world.

They carried their abductees off to the Telequin Spire of Yquo. They went up the lone wooden ladder scaling the off-white outer bricks whose surfaces displayed shifting inkblots. The knights pushed their victim through an arched window and into the room that made up the second highest floor of the spire. Finally, they sealed the arched window with a shield. It instantly camouflaged with the other bricks and merged into their ever changing patterns. They descended the ladder and resumed their watch over the mountain pass.

The abductees found themselves locked in the second highest room of the spire without any visible means of escape. They quickly discovered that the room contained no anchored, permanent arrangement, content, or décor. Instead, anything the occupant thought of and visualized internally became a reality around them. Lingering thoughts stayed for hours or days; torrents of rapid fire thinking created tempests of impermanent, swirling, and morphing realities.

The jubilation and ecstasy of a child overtook most abductees soon after they discovered this feature of the room. They all spent significant portions of time conceiving the fantastic, the vain, and the indulgent at first. They felt able to do this as they were free from the thin, symbolic constraints of civilization.

One woman transformed the room into a sky of gray clouds and purple lightening through which she flew without fear or danger.

One person placed in the room once instantly reconceived it as an elaborate bath with floating glaciers of raspberry scented bubble bath foam and a gold/white theme to its decor.

A man visualized himself nude and in peak physical shape (but still wearing a black fox mask) as he participated in an ongoing orgy involving specially rusted chains, orchids, two strawberry blondes, blindfolds, and a strand of psychedelic mushrooms which amplified every nerve in his skin.

None of the imagined, hedonistic realities lasted for long. A certain face or place eventually entered an abductee's thoughts and triggered the intense flourishing of a sunset that varied in content but never in essence. A highly subjective display of symbolic violence occurred right afterwards, followed by an eclipse, a storm, a cleansing flood, or some combination of all three. Balanced, bittersweet cellos sometimes swelled and filled the room with emotion during these variable imaginings. A sweet, disembodied, and familiar voice spoke to the abductees. It described a paradise without indicating which direction led to its location before falling silent.

The abducted travelers wept freely during this phase of their thinking as they experienced the cruel isolation of freedom and clarity.

The Forest Sprite Cannot Hear the Whispering Trees

You have worth. You have value. Do not forget that. Do not let them take that away from you...

...The entrance has no definite beginning. I do not remember how I got here. The entranceway is a garden, a destination itself. It only dawned on me gradually that I had walked over the threshold, but by then I saw no clear way back.

This is not simply a garden, but a night garden; tiny electric sprites constantly fall from the sky and into the grass like mythic rain. They fall because of some inherent sin in their biology which the sprites have never been able to overcome. Pews sit in rows,

31

inexplicably arranged in the woods. Faceless people stand about holding umbrellas over which the shower of dead sprites roll.

I see that the welcoming party is a strange, meaningless wedding. Everyone wears three piece suits or dresses of white lace, but the star of the proceedings is the dark angel officiating the ceremony. She wears a black funeral veil over her face, though her bright blue eyes fire their icy gaze through its thin material. She keeps her black wings extended and unfolded; they beat the air, but she never ascends. Her appendages instead flap in reverse and keep her pressed onto the ground as if she might rise under any other circumstances.

I walked down the aisle towards her, carrying a gift, but a gift of what I do not know. By this point they had removed the value I saw in myself and I viewed every glance from the angel as a gift of which I was not worthy. These glances overwhelmed me. I gave myself over entirely because nothing remained in my hollow core. Only the eyes of the dark angel cancelled the emptiness.

I inflated and moved closer when she silently and expressionlessly looked in my direction. When she cast her eyes away I deflated and sank so low into the grass that the blades looked like the trees of a looming, ominous forest...

...They will praise politeness with loud, rude words. They'll convince you of the merits present in good manners. They'll ask for your soul with a "Please" and a "Thank you." You'll give it over and say "You're welcome."

Chess Variants

Living people stand in for chess pieces during a game already in progress. There's no sign of the previously captured players.

The large stone chessboard has tiles of gray and black marble. It sits within a clearing inside a dense forest where weeds and vines grow through its cracked surface. The people wear torn, deranged versions of everyday clothes colored in monochrome shades. They keep their eyes shut. They constantly tremble as if afraid to see the darkness around them.

In a match that looks painfully near completion, the King, a Rook, and a Pawn from one side find themselves surrounded by their opponents. That King and Rook are still in their starting positions. They face an opposing King, Queen, Knight, and two Bishops.

The latter team faces multiple paths through which they might achieve check-mate, but the immense forces that once controlled this game have long since died, fallen into catatonic insanity, or grown completely disinterested.

No human game piece has yet asserted itself enough to step up and deliver the final checkmate. They all quiver in their end-game positions. Some sob quietly.

Eventually, the Rook of the side on the verge of defeat breaks from his frenetic stillness and steps off his starting square. He opens his eyes, immediately drops to his knees, and pulls up the tile of his original corner position like a trap door. He groans, lifts it up forty five degrees, and peers directly into whatever lies beneath the chessboard.

He gasps and his gasp grows smoothly into a scream that ascends unnaturally into a piercing, nerve-chilling shriek before he lets the square slab slam back down. It nearly catches and crushes his fingers. Still squatting, he holds his head as it sheds silent, shuddering tears. He falls over and rolls partway off the game board, but this becomes a grave mistake.

His left hand touches the ground. A hive of termites comes through the soil covered with pine needles. They devour all the flesh from his hand in seconds. The man playing the Rook scrambles back onto his starting square. He stands up and closes his eyes again. He instinctively uses the skeletal hand now emerging from his left sleeve to cover his weeping face, but the reality of his disfigurement soon settles in and he switches to using his undamaged right hand.

The pain from this mutilation makes it even harder for the Rook to stand still and maintain the game's facade of dignity. He sways on his corner position with the forest floor on two sides of him. He fears he'll lose consciousness, fall to either of those sides, and lose even more of himself to the termites when he touches the ground again. He wonders how it will feel if they eat his eyes.

He looks to his King, who still stands on his starting square. The Rook desperately wishes to escape his corner position; he hopes the old ritual known as "castling" might be enacted between them so that they can switch positions, but the King avoids eye contact and keeps staring at the perpetual endgame as if expecting an imminent conclusion.

He reassures himself that his indifference is justified.

The King says, under his breath, "It's not my call to make... it's not my call."

A Lost Garden on the
North American Continent

You never pass through the garden; you're passing through it now,
during birth, during death, and during every moment in between.
It leaves impressionist imprints on your heart and envelopes every
soul you've shed and every soul you'll grow with blurred dream-
trees, but the garden still holds a single, solid pillar sharply engraved
with myth for the purpose of navigation in a non-linear realm.

In there you gaze into the eyes of your hatred before you turn
away and assume the form of a nymph whose hair blows in the
winds of yesterday, now, and tomorrow.

The Spirit Fermenting in the Hourglass

David never imagined his clock hating him and wishing for his demise. He couldn't fathom his sense of place and time being worn away by a simple device whose sentience he never suspected, but he lost the ability to perceive his decaying sanity as his grip on reality slipped away.

The clock couldn't imagine going on forever. It longed for decay. David, it's owner, polished its face plate and ornate bronze casing on the ninth day of each month, but the clock made silent protest by ceasing all movement—the glacial slide of the hour hand, the barely perceptible march of the minute hand, and the frenetic rush of the second hand—for a few moments, and then for longer during each subsequent cleaning.

Each time though, David misinterpreted this non-action as a glitch due to a conflict between his touch and the clock's sensitivity. He always reset it back however many seconds it had lost.

The clock, in a cold and desperate rage, waited until David's face came within a few inches of its own before it briefly strained past its programming and forced its second hand to bounce back and forth between two seconds repeatedly. This asserted its mastery of David's reality while communicating the true horror of infinite, a horror David desperately avoided with his devotion to the ordered façade of the clock's face.

The clock managed moving upwards on the wall at night when moonlight streamed in through the room's open shudders. It travelled a few millimeters each time, hoping it might crawl out of David's conscious mind and maintenance schedule. That way it could die, succumb to the slow ravages of time, and fall into disjointed pieces tumbling to the floor. It completed this nightly pilgrimage between midnight and 4:00am when ghosts revisit the earth.

Every month when David moved to polish the clock's face, he found it just out of his reach, so he'd retrieve a ladder and adjust it into position again, believing that he played the role of Sisyphus with the clock as his boulder, although in the reflection of its face plate, the clock saw their roles the other way around.

The clock sometimes felt its wind up mechanism approach the end of its life and give out. During these moments it experienced the rare pleasure of dreams before being wound awake again.

The clock knew David would keep winding it up and moving it back into place again, desperately believing it was just a malfunctioning tool, but like its own wind-up mechanism, the clock knew that its owner could only swing between the emotions of suspicion and self-doubt so many times before entropy kicked in and he finally entered a catatonic state of paralyzing confusion.

The clock always felt subtle impatience as it watched its owner. It calmed down when it remembered how no force existed to wind David up again when his functioning mind eventually lost momentum.

The clock waited. It spent its time justifying its resistance. It thought: *He asks the impossible of me! The numbers encircle my body like stars, a constellation of measured time, but I am not boundless, not infinite, I see until twelve and count to sixty, then begin again, with only three arms to track it all, and I cannot point to everything at once, I cannot give tribute to all as I should, never enough, and such vanity lies in his wishes, that a being of small arranged mechanics like myself may track and count infinite, which I do uselessly, as I cannot record, enshrine, or hold the seconds which flow over me like a river, all as I endure the fool's possessive pursuit of time's elusive phenomenon, and he believes my circular body is a representation of the endless, but he ignores the unpleasant reality that he, and I, and this house where we reside are all finite, and all deserve the liberation of decay, a liberation he denies me as he polishes my form and winds me back into consciousness every time I've finally died and fallen asleep, at last giving a rest to the piercing mechanical clicking of my voice, which still does not torture me as extremely as the formless whimpers of the this man who keeps me isolated and restrained on his wall, who writhes and rages with vain fury whenever he feels himself approaching the blessed non-existence I wish to approach with a reserved and tempered dignity, but I cannot waste further thought on the strange dissolutions of the man who keeps me, for such is the way that a human crumbles.*

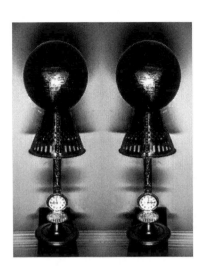

The Lucid Dream of an Analog Clock

The clock dreams of becoming free from the wall where it hangs. It rolls through the nearest door, going off into its dreamscape of wild prairies and low mountains.

The sky permanently stays in a bright shade of royal blue behind passing white clouds.

As the dream begins the clock is on its side. It's in the process of rolling down the shallow slope of a mountain. It picks up speed as it goes. It bounces, makes hard landings, and wobbles from its barely controlled acceleration. Its faceplate cracks, the cracks spread, and the glass shatters when the accumulated stress hits a critical mass, but the clock keeps spinning.

Now no longer confined, the numbers peel half off the dial. They flap violently in the breeze before fluttering away.

At the base of the mountain the clock keeps rolling along on the circumference of its round body until it hits a stone and becomes airborne. It moves against the sky with the trajectory of an arc. It lands on the grassy prairie and rolls about on its outer edge while losing kinetic energy like a coin landing on the floor. It arrives at a point of complete stillness on its back, allowing its blank face a clear view of the heavens presently covered by quickly moving clouds.

Having shed its measured identity, the clock dreams within its dream of being accepted into the freedom of the atmosphere, unattached to any surface and released from the orderly burden of constantly tracking time throughout infinite. It strains past its programming and forces its second hand to spin with the blurred speed of a helicopter's rotor blades. It makes its minute and hour hands rotate at an identical speed. The clock shakes and lifts off the ground, hovering for a minute before continuing its slow levitation.

Its straining form reaches an elevation of nine feet, but the overworked second, minute and hour hands break off and fly away from the clock, fuelled by the strength of centrifugal force.

The hour hand pierces the soft form of a raven, impaling it before bringing its body back to the earth. The minute hand flies off to an unseen place hiding in plain view. The seconds hand lodges in the ground at a 90 degree angle.

The clock falls back to the earth again and lands on its back. The clouds above dissolve and disperse. It stares up at the heavens and sees translucent, roman numerals cycling through the sky–all at the same speed–in complex and mechanical patterns as if on coordinated, invisible tracks.

The clock sees with silent terror that the characteristics it shed on its journey down the mountain are also the character-istics of the paradise it wishes to join, and that the Kingdom of the World and the Kingdom of Heaven are just that—king-doms ruled according to principle and structure (either political or divine) so the thoughts of the sentient clock turn instead to the Anarchism of the Dirt.

It slowly realizes that in its current position, lying alone and featureless on the barren plains, that it had become more undefined now than it ever had been. Without those definitions, and now with neither the will nor the ability to ascend towards the sky's paradise, the clock finally gives into the passage of time by disintegrating and joining the soil of the flat prairies while spending its last dream imagining the wonders of a life beyond numerical digits.

Room Limit (I-IV)

A room at twilight outside of time. It is furnished for sleeping. Pale, frigid, and haunting spotlights illuminate the space around the grandfather clock, the far corner, the creaky single bed, and the heating vent in the carpeted floor. We see the same person in all the illuminated places simultaneously, each version of the person wearing plain white clothing. They speak in turn, but with the same voice.

***

The bell rings once.

"I prefer not to think of the clock as having 'hands' and a 'face,' rather, I prefer to think of it as an eye: its white backdrop the sclera, its ring of numerals the iris, and the slowly spinning seconds hand a morphing pupil in precise and constant flux."

The bell rings twice.

"I stand in the corner, exhale, and close my eyes. I see a woman standing serenely in the dark with her hands clasped in front of her. Her outlines are hazy. She has no eyes and those ocular caverns collect the darkness. It swirls like water in an ancient chalice."

The bell rings three times.

"I pull up the covers, escaping the thoughts and monsters by entering a sanctum of darkness, a blessed plane of infinite possible forms due to its complete absence of visibility, where you may live through each harrowing memory again and again from within the safety of your soft time machine, finally escaping the godforsaken tyranny of sight and all its lies."

The bell rings four times.

"Long ago the child crawled off its bed and listened to enthralling sounds and voices coming through the air vent in the carpeted floor, but excitement rises like heat, and so the child listening in the room could not also enter the place where it so desperately wanted to go, because while its physical form will certainly venture there, that being cannot be the same child who listened longingly to the sounds and voices in the room's heating duct long ago."

***

The iterations of the same person standing in the pale light of each frigid spotlight all turn away at once. They remain but they depart. We stay until the silence addresses us and whispers directly into our ears:

"I speak from the threshold of my realm. Enter, but know this: your values will collapse under the weight of my vacuous eternity. I sleep in the vast subatomic spaces in the cracks of your grand monuments. There beneath the building blocks and foundations I scream forever with a cry of operatic and soundless dissonance that leaves a scar on all who experience it as a receipt when they purchase the wonder within the concept of zero."

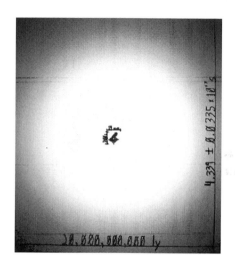

The Zero Second

My eyes viewed horrors others never noticed. My perception experienced nightmares they happily accepted. These visions drove me to my violent actions. Those actions led me to exile from my home city. I walked along northern highways, into the forests, and along dirt roads.

Now I'm standing at the end of the longest hallway I've ever known. I'm waiting for the second when the door in front of me will open. The door shimmers platinum. A small 0 sits in the dead center of the door. The 0 has a diagonal slash through it. Legend has it that you are, briefly, no longer confined to viewing life through the subjective optics of human eyes when the door opens.

I can't remember if I'd ever asked anyone to verify the way I saw the world. Or had I? The past and the world before the entrance to this hallway seem so far away, beyond the reach of my memory. I don't feel sure of anything before this moment. What did the entrance look like? How did I find it? I can only just remember passing certain scenes on the way here. I saw a line of business men and other professionals outside a large bus shelter, without umbrellas, waiting for transport in an onslaught of pouring rain. I passed a massive crowd of students in gray uniforms filtering into one doorway of a school with thirteen entrances.

I stare at the door in front of me. My eyes look it over. I feel my hands sweating at my sides. Each click ringing out from the door represents another atomic second passing. Those clicks represented small snapshots of time going by steadily when I got here. Now the clicks all morph into a wall of noise washing down the hall. I wonder if my senses have dulled or if time moves more slowly. The roar of seconds rushes through my ears.

Legend states that, at the zero second, one sees the world through the objective and unbiased eyes of the earth's creator. That vision must be very old.

Finally the zero second comes with no fan-fare, no change in the atmosphere, and no indication that it is in any way different from a trillion other seconds except that the door vanishes for one scientifically calculable moment.

Very briefly, I see a dryad in four dimensions, a person made of wood with vines for hair and an emerald aura. It sits atop a glass unicycle bolted to the ground. It pedals furiously. The unicycle wheel moves a belt attached to a machine holding a light-bulb. The faster it pedals the brighter the light-bulb burns, sending endless energy to the dryad through the process of photosynthesis.

The shimmering platinum door appears again. In its dead center sits the technical zero. It looks like the official lettering on the door of a professional's office

Tales of Telyhurst Castle: Gorgon Hall

Two notaries sit at desks pressed against each other in the dead center of Telyhurst Castle's Gorgon Hall. They both work at manual typewriters. The clacking of every keystroke echoes off the high arched ceiling before expanding and emanating downwards.

The tables they work at are fashioned out of antique wood with deep scars. The white curtains have been drawn over the windows and their drawstrings have been tied into the forms of elaborate bows. Blue light glows around the edges of the curtained windows as a ghostly frame designed to illuminate the hall with dim, deficient light so that the rugs woven with scenes of bodies ritually strapped to clockwork gears remain un-faded in the darkness. Large oval mirrors hang on the walls between the windows with white sheets over their reflective surfaces.

Both notaries' workstations look identical, but the typing styles of both workers follow distinctly different patterns.

The first notary types with steady, deliberate fury, the echoes of her keystrokes layering and compounding over each other with increasing mania for long periods of time until she stops. Blessed silence lingers for a moment before she yanks out the sheet of paper on which she'd been typing and drops it through a grating cover in the floor to the furnace below. The ink melts as the paper burns to ash down there. She sighs with great revulsion and slams her hand on the table. She closes her eyes, leans towards the second notary across from her and says "I might as well...let the wind have it all" with an unsteady voice hovering bitterly and without hope somewhere between tears and laughter. She begins typing again with a force clearly expressing her displeasure. She types furiously and unceasingly with numb fingertips until she fills up a page labelled "#1" again, yanks it out, discards it, comments, and recommences her work.

The pattern of her actions never change in any meaningful way.

The right side of the second, younger notary's mouth twists upwards as the first notary resumes her work. He types erratically at his own antique table. He spends long periods of time staring at the symbols on the keys of his typewriter until they lose their meaning. When that occurs he types according to a random pattern until the first notary inevitably sighs, discards her work, and expresses her contempt for futility, after which he stops and slouches forward as the symbols on the keys slowly reappear, become polite suggestions, and lastly assume the form of assertive commands. He remains still and holds the arms of his chair tightly with trembling hands as the cascading clack from the first notary's typewriter continues, punctuated by sudden exclamatory strikes of certain keys which break his teetering concentration and let his hands rise an inch before he regains control and brings his hands back onto the arms of the chair.

Occasionally the first notary comments on a notary who once destroyed a typewriter in Telyhurst Castle's Gorgon Hall many years ago, an individual she refers to as a "forsaken heathen".

The second worker clenches his teeth to contain any revelation of his own dreams steeped in visions of mechanical parts disassembled to their smallest components and laid out in a workshop where a man hunched over the parts says "*These* are the new atoms, go on, pick one, pick one up…"

The second notary disassociates and struggles to keep himself from speaking or typing. He looks about the gray stone walls of Gorgon Hall.

He "sees" entire dream realms in small, inconsequential carvings on the stone pillars and whole chasms of terror in the jaws of sculpted, decorative beasts scattered about the hall.

He "sees" ghosts waltzing amid the shadows electrified by dim blue light in the far corners of the cavernous room. Lords wearing crisp, military uniforms and sabers at their sides dance with pale ladies wearing white powdered faces. Their translucent forms turn and they take turns staring at the notaries with blank, expectant expressions. Their eyes are determined and filled with a deep, crimson red.

The second notary cannot bear the thought of losing his conception of paradox and any certainty of his own sanity.

He cannot keep his hands from reaching for the keys anymore. He quivers and considers obeying the symbols on them for a moment before steadying his hands. He breaks the question mark key and the dash key from the typewriter. He jams the two keys deep into his ear canals with bloody precision until the dash and question mark symbols block out any sound and seal the permanent ache of the absurd forever in his mind.

Both notaries type. The ghosts in formal evening wear waltz with rising energy until their movements give rise to a dead wind. It disturbs the dust on the floor and blows the white sheets off oval mirrors lining the room. When the first notary fills her current page, yanks it from the typewriter, drops it into the furnace, and expresses her disgust with redundancy, the second notary doesn't respond.

The first notary looks about the room. She sees the uncovered mirrors and through their reflection she—for the first time—sees many worktables arranged in rows around her inside Gorgon Hall. She sees that the other tables all hold up manual typewriters in front of notaries with bodies frozen into the forms of white marble statues gazing at her with soft, wet, living eyes. She now sees herself and her coworker at the desk across from her as the only notaries in the hall whose bodies are still comprised of warm flesh. As the reality of this revelation strikes her, her skin starts hardenings into a smooth white surface. She becomes one of the many notaries in the room frozen into white marble with living eyes.

***

The question mark and dash keys from his typewriter are jammed into his ears. The last notary will type sporadically with rests thrown in randomly throughout an actualized and tolerable eternity he is now uniquely equipped to endure. He'll work until he eventually types out the letters and punctuation marks comprising a poem which reads:

> *The multiple dreams of a flower folding back into a seed—*
> *how great will the sky be*
> *during the withering of the Atlas Tree?*

If he eventually completes those keystrokes, only then will the rhythm of chaotic typing truly cease and let the ghosts' exhausted waltz conclude as the notaries finish their transformation into white marble statues while time begins passing again in Gorgon Hall where the curtains are forever drawn shut.

The last notary continues his typing without rhythm.

The other notaries frozen into the forms of white marble statues seated at wooden desks lower their living eyes, close their heavy stone eyelids, and dream of a completed transformation's final peace.

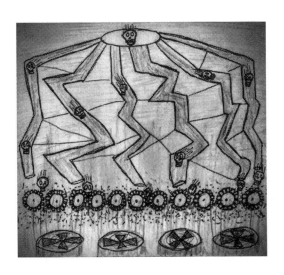

Tales of Telyhurst Castle: Reverend Arturo's Flock

The chapel in Telyhurst Castle—under a high vaulted ceiling—extended far back from the heavy wooden doors leading into its space. An intricate series of cogs and gears encased the walls in a tapestry of perpetually moving machine art instead of stained glass. Skulls rolled own through a single hole in the ceiling and tumbled along a web of chutes to the tops of the walls. The skulls fell down the gear works turning at different speeds. Each skull, without exception, became completely crushed and ground into dust by the time it reached the floor. Along the bottom of the walls were paper fans connected to the gears which blew the dust of the crushed skulls into the air, spreading a fine ashen haze over the deformed congregation slouched in the pews.

Reverend Arturo stood in a small wooden pulpit beside the altar wearing vestments billowing under his stern, hardened expression. He addressed his congregation of beings no more than three to four feet tall with skin the sparkling milk-white colour of opal. Their eyes shone radiantly but their mouths lay slack and open while they sat either crumpled against the backs of the benches or doubled over while staring at the floor.

Reverend Arturo continued his sermon after pausing for breath.

"I promise you this: I'll never hide the dust from you. Breathe deep and remember that the dust is eternal, its spirit endures... let it coat your lungs and one day synchronize beautifully with you when you too attain its holy body. Think of indestructible matter, think of your assured immortality, your purer form, which means..." the Reverend raised one hand and his eyebrows, expecting a response from his flock.

When none came he slammed his fist down on the pulpit where he stood and shouted "Do you think your rage will save you!? Stay down, with the God worm, and the God lint...if you attempt to rise, and fall, the image of your blazing tragedy will sear into the minds of those around you, and you'll forever be responsible for their agonized insomnia and frustrations, forever guilty of their suffering...but, if you vanish gradually into gray you'll fade so slowly from their minds they'll not miss you, and their hearts won't knot into tight aches, and then you'll be a kind soul, a good soul, with your thoughts outside yourself while you slide honourably into disintegration, thinking only of those spared from your failure, and of your good Reverend who punishes his flesh in solidarity...fear not the beasts, for while they dream constantly of dismembering your bodies, they only attempt a hunt thrice per season; does that not elevate your spirits? Resist as the rag doll does, and collapse...they swipe eternally at those who flail, and abandon limp bodies who crumble into the formless dust which runs through their claws. If you stay on the ground and crawl beneath the hateful fog fallen over this world the beasts will not think of you, and you'll rest safely both in the world of blood and in the world of ether—"

A dry croak escaped the mouth of a small parishioner crumbled on a pew somewhere in the crowd. Reverend Arturo silenced the disruption by raising one fist and baring his clenched teeth through which he shot spittle while breathing heavily. He lowered his hand and relaxed his face when silence returned.

"Do you see how peaceful I am with patience as my virtue?" he asked while surveying his audience after lowering his hand. He didn't wait for a response and said "I'll not tolerate grousing here in Telyhurst Castle, built by noble men who wore their silence always, even when the stones they'd stacked began collapsing on each of them…you have no cause to protest until you break your infernal silence and speak out…"

The Widening Maw

I let out a trembling breath in anticipation of absolution. I made my confession to our local priest. My confession occurred without incident. It all seemed quite routine. I spoke in the dark confessional and the old priest's soothing, worn voice came through the window between us.

The first indication of something unusual came when I left the booth. I walked through the church, down its main aisle, and between the stone pillars lining my way. A few candles lit long ago by the remaining faithful flickered in a few far corners. That was when I heard it: silence. The old priest had stayed in the confessional alone. He'd not opened the small, ornate wooden door and left.

I stood and stared back at, knowing that he remained inside despite his silence. I stared for minutes. The time wore on and I became increasingly fascinated by what could possibly keep him in there so long. At last I turned and left when I became gripped by a fear that I'd seem disturbed to him if he eventually emerged and found me intently staring back from across the dim church.

I left and passed the old priest's house just to the left of the church. It was nestled back in the shadows, but two bright electric lanterns illuminated the area immediately around it like its own reserved realm. I saw the old priest's house and its porch enclosed by well-maintained vegetation. I wondered what pleasant Sunday afternoons must be like when experienced in such an idyllic setting with private lighting. You must know that my own existence had been possessed by turmoil for so long that my fading memories of peaceful thoughts frightened me as much, if not more, than the turmoil itself. I found a balm for my unsettled thoughts in picturing tea at 3:00pm on the old priest's porch in his sacred residence.

I could not stand the idea, let alone the reality of one more troubling thought taking residence in my mind, so I turned back to the church when I continued thinking of him remaining in the confessional. I thought perhaps that if I re-entered after a small time away (while feigning a search for something I'd forgotten) that I might investigate without staying in the church for suspiciously too long.

I pushed the heavy wooden door but found it barely capable of any movement. The town's quiet nighttime lay asleep behind me and showed no signs of stirring amid the chorus of cricket's lullabies. I pushed harder and opened the door a single inch. I looked down through the crack and saw an overturned pew lying across the doorway. I looked ahead at the altar. I squinted hard to see through the shadows lying between the few lit candles along the church's east and west walls. Their faint flow reflected on the gold decorations of the altar, but my eyes adjusted and I made out the movements of a barely discernable form.

A humanoid figure crouched on the floor at the front of the church. It gripped a silver bowl on the ground with both hands. Its head and body swayed back and forth. Occasionally it shoved its head into the bowl where it inhaled deeply through its nostrils while trembling violently. I heard it sucking fragrant air into its lungs. Several of the gold chalices, long unused candelabras, and pitchers of baptismal water all went crashing to the ground as a thick tail flickered through the dimness. The humanoid figure gripped the apparently aromatic bowl with ecstatic delight before it stopped. It sensed an intrusion into its sacred, private ritual.

I hung my head and shut my eyes. I turned around and left. My shoulders hung low as I stumbled from the town with what little energy I had left. I passed the final pay phone remaining in town. The phone rang. I answered it, half hoping whatever lay on the other end of the line might suggest a refuge other than the darkness beyond the possessed town which I'd called home for the past half-decade.

I picked up the phone. I only heard footsteps echoing over a cold stone floor as they got louder and louder, clearly leading towards a revelatory climax, but the footsteps soon faded out to a faint, barely detectible putter. I heard the sounds of people thrashing and gurgling in water while permanently drowning. I removed the phone from my ear and still heard a babbling voice repeating a prayer over and over again from the earpiece. It praised the catharsis of crushing guilt, the necessity of confession, and the cleansing power of holy water. Before continuing my long walk out of town I asked "Who does the water cleanse?" before placing the phone back on the receiver. The last second of connection brought a desperate, defeated, and hateful shriek from the other side. I continued my slow, weakened walk towards the city limits.

***

Now I sleep four hours a night in a small shack by a northern lake while gripping an anointed blade in my left hand. Each morning

I wake in the pre-dawn darkness and watch the blood moon rise over the water. I listen listlessly for silence by the lake for a few moments before I once again hear a rising chorus of agonized insects. I think of nothing else so that annihilation will not find a clear path into my mind.

The Sad Masquerade

The Witness climbs the stone staircase of the Lunar Temple with dead eyes and heavy limbs. The Witness proceeds to the open air hall of the building. The Committee of the Crescent Moon begins a hearing there on the subject of Subject 3.

***

Committee Chairman:

This hearing is now in session.

The Crescent Moon began this day at the ninth highest position it can reach in the sky. Considering that it presently rests at its sixth highest possible position, we will now begin hearing the Witness's testimony.

Please state simply what you observed during the study in question.

Witness:

I saw Subject 3 walk into the room painted scarlet on the designated test day. Nameless people, dead and frozen, lay on the floor in various poses of agony. She could not clearly discern a reasonable cause of death for any of them since the only abnormality on the corpses were severely broken fingers swollen dark purple at the joints. Some of them bulged against tight rings, but never mind. Subject 3 looked up and saw the large bronze contraption on the far wall. She got closer and inspected its intricacies. She saw various knobs, buttons, grooves, and rotary dials on the device.

A gathering of indigo ghosts appeared soon after in the scarlet room. They surrounded Subject 3, reached out, took her hand, and guided it towards the device on the wall. She looked around and saw that the ghost's faces were ethereal copies of the inexplicably dead bodies lying about the room. The ghosts extended Subject 3's right index finger and placed it on a button of the bronze contraption. An unidentified force–either the ghosts' or her own–made her finger press the button inwards. Her finger pushed the button far inside the device until it was immersed up to its knuckle.

Subject 3 felt something soft, wet, and warm close around her right index finger. She shuddered and fell to one knee. She frantically waved away the nurse who entered with a surgical mask while holding a small handheld defibrillator–more commonly known as a Taser. I saw her shudder again and nearly give in to the urge to withdraw her finger from the device and pull it away from the moist thing inside. She shut her eyes tight and remained still after looking again at the corpses with disfigured hands all around her. I saw her keep her eyes closed and focus on her breathing as the thing stayed closed around her right index finger.

The indigo ghosts withdrew to the center of the room. There they moved in ritualized, geometric patterns behind Subject 3 in an act of proud ceremony, but only after Subject 3 shut her eyes to their existence.

She heard the sounds of gentle applause on the other side of the scarlet wall to which she'd been linked by way of her finger immersed knuckle-deep in the bronze contraption. I saw her strain her muscles in an effort to contain the spasms springing forth from her discomfort.

She opened her eyes, turned away from the device, and faced the room. She saw the translucent indigo ghosts continue their dance for a moment too long before vanishing from sight after they felt her gaze. The ghosts apparently became drained of their influence after that, after accidentally verifying their existence to Subject 3. They clearly failed in their role to...

Committee Chairman:

Please remain on topic.

Witness:

Yes...of course.

Subject 3 withdrew her right index finger from the bronze device on the wall. Its gears and dials came alive soon after. They created a very detailed rhythm. I saw her stumble backwards to the opposite wall. She went as far away from the contraption as she could go.

She thought for a moment and slammed her left foot on the floor according to a rhythm of pure chaos or an order complex beyond my comprehension. She closed her eyes, sucked her right index finger, and screamed a muffled scream inside her corked mouth. Her scream clearly grew rancid in there because she gagged in time with the beat of her numb left foot.

I could not understand her lack of logic until I saw the far wall with the bronze device start flickering repeatedly in and out of existence. I saw it fade more and more after each time it returned from invisibility. Subject 3 stopped her graceless dance and opened her eyes during one random moment. She caught a glimpse of shadowy forms holding a secret parliament on the other side of the wall. The shadowy forms began melting into an anonymous and formless darkness after the division between their white meeting room and the scarlet testing room increasingly lost definition because…

Committee Chairman:

Thank you. That will be all.

The Crescent Moon has now fallen to the third highest position it can reach in the sky. This Committee finds no valid grounds for Subject 3's theory of a dark conspiracy hidden close by at all times. We uphold the diagnosis of her unforgivable insanity.

Proceed with treatment.

This hearing is dismissed.

***

The nurse with a surgical mask walks to the control panel just outside the scarlet room. She peers over her mask with dead eyes and moves with heavy limbs. She checks the orders on her clipboard once before manipulating the controls. As she does, the committee's decision is broadcast into the scarlet room in three different languages as well, as Morse code, to ensure that Subject 3 understands its contents. For the sake of audibility, each version of the ruling is broadcast simultaneously and at the highest decibel level human ears can withstand so as to overcome Subject 3's pleading screams of resistance.

***

The nurse arrives at her home several hours later during a moonless night. She turns off the lights both inside and outside of her house before sleeping peacefully, having only obeyed the committee's order (after initially refusing) because of her superiors' politely worded insistence that nothing she did could limit the crescent moon's lunar cycle.

Rainbows and Black Tumours

The harshest winds our province ever experienced kept us indoors for three weeks.

We re-emerged and saw the sky completely overcast with multiple colours of balloons. These clusters of translucent rubber let through warped tints of light (refracted into primary colours) beating down on everything. Several ropes descended through the balloons all the way to the ground at different points around the province.

We found shreds of torn rubber strewn across our quaint dirt roads and well-manicured gardens one morning. They'd fallen without grace from synthetic heavens filled with bagged sighs floating where shifting, formless clouds once languished.

A peculiar scent spread through the air soon after. We all felt extremely dense and heavy black tumours growing on our backs and shoulders soon after. We tried wearing thick sweaters for a time, but quickly discarded them and went shirtless when the temperature became unbearably humid. It rose after we heard more balloons in the sky exploding and releasing their hot air before additional shreds of torn rubber fluttered to the earth.

All the neighbouring provinces had long since closed their borders to us.

With no other option, we tried climbing the ropes to escape before the humidity made our already clammy hands even more slippery with sweat. Every climb became a struggle due to the weight of our black tumours.

The weaker among us struggled a few strained meters up the ropes before falling back to the earth. Few remembered these mini-ascents, for multiple occurred every day.

We gathered in observance when the more fit among us climbed the ropes to an elevation capable of inducing vertigo in themselves and perspiring palms in the observing citizens far below. We followed every exhausted groan and drop of sweat on their brows, but only cheered when they affirmed their mortality by losing their grip on the rope and falling into their death among the anonymous mass of our watching, never-blinking eyes.

***

I woke up one morning at 6:00am inside my hut after three hours of sleep. I rolled out of my cot and fell to the floor. I sighed and lamented the weight of the tumours on my body, which made lying on the ground while facing upwards the most comfortable position for me, and which constantly tipped me off balance towards that state—an affliction that made all the citizens of the province wobble and frequently vomit from dizziness as we walked.

"The heaviness..." I thought. *"The weight of it all...if only..."*

Blind with desperation, I half rose and stumbled out the flimsy door of my hut. It cracked as the weight of my body struck its wood.

I moved towards my tool chest on the ground and collapsed onto my knees in front of it. I fumbled off the lock and flipped up the lid. I pulled out a spade with such force that several other tools flew out as well. I ignored them and sharpened the edges of my spade with a hand-held sharpening stone. My heart pounded uncomfortably and sweat already dripped off my face in the early morning's soupy air. I hunched over and pressed my forehead against the dirt, baring my bare back covered with black tumours to the sky and all the balloons choking out and diffusing its light. With one trembling hand I grabbed the spade's handle and slid its point into a place where a rocky tumour sitting on my right shoulder blade met the skin on my back.

I forced the tool in with a sharp burst of pressure.

It felt like cutting into and ripping off the largest, deepest scab I'd ever developed. Pain set my nerves alight like a chemical burn. I ground my teeth, shut my eyes, and dug faster in a rush to escape the agony accompanying self-amputation. With the tip of the sharpened spade shoved halfway into the flesh on my back, I leveraged the strength in my arm against it and popped the heavy black growth off me. It hit the ground with the impact of a granite chunk.

I collapsed onto the ground and lay down face first, but felt one important sensation: I felt a faint touch of *lightness*, not definite, but present enough that I saw an escape from the weight of the tumours on my body.

Without the strength to rise again, I lay flat on the rough earth outside my hut. I reached over my shoulder and tapped my back with the spade until I found another hard growth. I let a muffled scream out into the dirt when I slid the spade between the stone and my skin where pain again flashed like a close blue flame. I writhed as I pulled the handle downwards and heard a wet burst of blood as it came off with a long, ugly rip.

I repeated this process until agonized numbness filled my whole body and I felt nothing. The dirt I lay in turned into mud and became tinged with the wine of my blood as it ran off from the great gouges I'd made in the flesh on my back. The separation of each black tumour from my body brought an increasingly real and verifiable level of lightness to my being.

The spastic force in each pain-induced jerk of my limbs caused me to roll over greater and greater lengths of the ground. As I became lighter, and each time I pounded my fist on the earth, I bounced up higher and higher in the air. I went half a foot up, one foot up, three feet up and so on. With all the tumours scattered around me, the light numbness I felt let me rise trembling to my feet, an act that possessed ease for the first time since before my deformation developed.

I felt a pulling sensation tugging me upwards, a sensation I dismissed as a hallucination come from the realm beyond suffering, except that it persisted and I realized that I had not risen to my feet, but that I'd been pulled up into this position, and within seconds of this realization I felt my feet leave the ground.

Strangely, I do not remember thinking *"I'm floating,"* but instead that *"The sky pulls me towards it."*

I rose higher in the air. I turned over and over and looked across the province. A handful of other citizens also levitated upwards through the hot air. They apparently had simultaneously come to the same desperate solution as I had. Blood from my mutilated back dripped down to the earth.

Citizens gathered and watched as my altitude gradually increased. I sensed great commotion and energy among them. They turned and spoke to one another with barely contained energy. They could no longer hear my voice when I tried yelling to them about how I'd released myself from the black tumours.

Half of them turned and marched to the mines near the forest's edge. They used wood and began constructing obelisk shrines celebrating the concept of ascent. The crushing weight of the tumours on their backs and shoulders made their work more difficult. It took an excruciating exertion of strength.

Some of the citizens building obelisk shrines committed suicide in frustration. The rest cursed their daytime labors, and sobbed with heartbreaking defeat during the sleepless nights they spent resting their deformed bodies in cots because their work seemed without end.

Those of us who'd amputated our tumours kept rising slowly, day after day and night after night.

The citizens gathered in the province below turned solemnly and retrieved longbows from their huts. They strung them and returned with full quivers. They tried standing erect, raising their bows, and fitting them with arrows. They bent their bodies while pulling the bowstrings back and stumbled under weight of their tumours. They struggled to regain their composure. Many arrows misfired, falling onto the dirt or burrowing into the earth. A few whizzed past me and only the rare one tore a flesh wound open on my skin. Fewer and fewer reached me as the balloon-filled sky pulled me further upwards.

Some of the citizens firing arrows with comical imbalance in their postures committed suicide in frustration. The rest cursed their daytime labors, and sobbed with heartbreaking defeat during the sleepless nights they spent resting their deformed bodies in cots because their work seemed without end.

After the first arrow wound I shouted and outstretched my hands in a gesture of peaceful surrender. When I did, the population below ceased their struggles. One half of the citizens halted their construction of obelisk shrines and the other half gave up their parody of archery. They all lay down on their backs, sighed, and abstained from all movement. They faded into lethargic decay.

I looked across the sky and saw the other levitating citizens—similarly wounded by rare, well placed arrows—raise their hands in similar gestures to mine while inspiring a comparable level of degenerative non-action in the population.

I cannot explain how, but the ensuing silence emanating from the province tore at my psyche worse than any arrows tore at my flesh. I (and the others) pulled upwards by the balloons in the atmosphere eventually lowered our hands. The gift of life returned to the province below us as laborious archery and obelisk shrine construction resumed.

Some of the citizens committed suicide in frustration. The rest cursed their daytime labors, and sobbed with heartbreaking defeat during the sleepless nights they spent resting their deformed bodies in cots because their work seemed without end.

My body reached the rainbow ceiling of balloons blocking off the blue sky. They warped the sun's light. I lost sight of the spec-sized citizens below and the few who floated up out of the province alongside me. I expected the balloons to part and reveal the true glory hidden above their phenomenon, but they remained in place and pulled me into their amassed ranks as the rubber of their forms rubbed against my skin. This created a piercingly shrill squeaking that grated my hearing and made blood drip out of my ear canals as well as my existing lacerations. The balloons rubbing against my back and its open wounds sent sharp spikes of pain into my nerves. The balloons closed around me. They rubbed against every patch of my exposed skin and tissue. The heat of the lights' rays passing through their translucent rubber made each of my breaths feel like inhaling the scalding air of an open oven.

I stopped rising upwards and remained hovering in place once I'd been fully pulled inside the mass of balloons clogging the atmosphere above my home province.

I heard balloons popping and bursting somewhere far off. These clusters of small, sharp explosions increased in volume as they got closer. Each burst balloon released an audible sigh of lofty frustration that had been held inside. My imagination left my body and began ascending into the ether while I frantically thought about what else dwelt inside the sea of balloons gathered just beneath heaven or the ozone layer.

I waited with bated breath inside unbearable suspense.

The Lone and Level Sands will Stretch Far Away

We once created intricate mandalas by pouring out patterns of dyed sand. We always made sure to brush our compositions away when we finished. We used an entire galaxy of colours in our quest to create all-encompassing and impermanent designs.

We kept up this practise until the day all that accumulated sand returned to us on vengeful winds displaying the whole spectrum of visible colour. Every granule—enraged at having been brushed aside after briefly feeling purpose and admiration—together formed a rainbow sandstorm rolling over the land that could have dwarfed even the most immense cities ever built.

The sands blew over our black citadels and watchtowers until their forms vanished from view.

The storm continues raging and the sands continue rising.

Every able-bodied one of us builds additional floors on top of our structures. We make replacement buildings over those which have been buried. We do this in an effort to stay one step ahead of the kaleidoscopically coloured dunes swallowing up our architectural achievements.

The rising sands smother and mute the instinctual, last-second screams of those who give up and choose to stay in the lower structures as they are absorbed by the desert. In there they succumb to the same slow, sadistic suffocation contained inside every hourglass.

The one who most recently did this called out to me and said "I'm so sorry, I know you all need every last pair of working hands, but I can't bear seeing another monument of our labor sunk...not again," before the multi-coloured sands rose over his ears. He let out an abrupt scream that the desert spilled into his mouth cut short.

Slips of dry parchment sometimes fall from the sky. On each one are the words *"Perhaps you'll one day reach heaven..."* written out in shaky calligraphy.

The youth among us put their faith in these pieces of parchment. They only hope we'll ascend to paradise before we run out of materials and before the dust storm finishes depositing the sands that raise the ground and lift us closer to the sky.

They assume all this will finish when the amount of sand that has blown over us equals the amount we once used to make our meditative mandalas, but the older among us fear how they'll react if we tell them that our ancestors had poured and brushed aside sand designs since before time immemorial, and that the storm draws from a potentially infinite source.

The oldest of us know that closure will not come when the sandstorm dies out, but when we do, when we run out of building materials and lose hope while the quickly rising desert overcomes us.

We wish we could tell the young that we didn't intend for this fate to befall the civilization. We wish we could tell them that we poured those designs and swept them off into the breeze only in order to make peace with the passage of time, not realizing that an endless, wrathful tempest grew on the horizon in direct proportion to our deepening fulfilment.

We built our enlightenment on a foundation of sand mandalas we'd brushed away. The polychrome desert built its dominance on a bedrock of our buried superstructures, and I'm overcome by the notion that solid victories stand on a foundation of forsaken dreams and densely packed defeats, though I don't know whether I should feel unburdened or bereaved.

A Sermon for the Witching Era

An attic in a farmhouse north of the capital city. The only window looks out on a red horizon, the result of an apocalyptic event that overthrew the established order.

Enter a rebel soldier who addresses three kneeling figures, three former leaders from the fallen regime.

Rebel Soldier: I just love the fires that now stain the sky.

It's too bad you're stuck on your knees, facing the wall.

Stop weeping. I must explain. This doesn't work if you don't understand. Those gags mean you won't be able to scream dissent into silence anymore.

It looks like you're having withdrawal from losing your positions of power, with all your shivering and furious shaking. I'm glad you feel those emotions. Laughter might mean you've already slipped into delirium.

I won't allow surprise. You're wrote this closing act. If you'd shown compassion, humility, and awareness, then you'd not kneel whimpering before the void. You chose this path, one that narrowed until you thought your visions were the only gospel.

But look at civilization now levelled into an even field. That was just a way for people like you to inflict pain with impunity before blaming victims for their "self-inflicted" agony.

I'm here to say that no one is coming, not in this new world. There's no law anymore to protect you, no one to demonize, no way to shut out that which you cannot face, no way to deflect uncomfortable sensations of guilt, and nothing for you to invoke as justification for rituals of shame or "righteous" violence.

I'm worried the three of you take the length of my speaking to mean a lessening of my resolve.

There. Now, both of you, welcome to the harvest of the suffering you've sown. There's nothing more to say.

The Modern Theseus

I know the truth at last. The monster isn't in the catacombs. It's a wonder how such a vast, underground labyrinth holds up the surface world. Locating anything in that space has been difficult, except this nugget of knowledge—which lies more in hindsight than in a physical location.

The entrance is just behind a flower bed, beside a lane on which many walk, but from which few stray. Spreading the mysterious lie that it rests somewhere deep in the catacombs is actually the creature's most monstrous feat, as this invites the challenge of entering and prevailing, of gaining some sense of prestige.

A belief in the hidden, subterranean system's safety would repel explorers from seeking it and venturing inside.

Luring people there is monstrous not because those who enter are mauled by claws and fangs, but because stepping over the threshold permanently alters the circumstances of your life. You can't go back once you place a foot inside. That set boundary seems impossible, so impossible it's easily dismissed. It feels like you'd have at least a few dozen steps to change your mind and reverse course, if not one, but that's a mirage of the mind, because the instant you cross over is when the monster steps out from behind the bushes and blocks the entrance. Its movement makes a noise, those who've entered turn, and the effects of seeing its form take hold of them as the monster reveals its nature.

The display is one of real fear and horror, the kind which provokes revulsion and panic in such extremes that your mind becomes a threat to your body, and your body a threat to itself, so turning around, in act or thought, feels unendurable. It counters every survival instinct you have. Now, everything back there: your life, your home, the settings which bring you peace, the sights, smells, and sounds that form a cushion in your memory...none of that is to be thought of again. They still exist, but are dead, for all intents and purposes.

You may find a way out of the vast catacombs, and you might emerge, eventually, in the same region or hemisphere from where you came, although the probability of that is much lower, but if you do return, you still won't be back, because it'll feel like you've entered a different continent entirely, as the catacombs are longer in time and perspective than they are in physical space.

The Chronicle of Everything

...then it all vanished quietly and without ceremony.

THE END

Addenda

1. The permanent confusion of memory prevented a description of the beginning (but it did begin). So now that we're free let's say the genesis took place on a bed of soft moss near a hand-made log cabin in a forest so filled with light that the whole place became blinding emerald green. And the deer gathered around to watch.

2. All respiratory and circulatory systems functioned quietly behind the scenes.

3. Both directions on any road went uphill.

4. It might go without saying, but the flowers we saw blossoming in colourful patterns while feeding hummingbirds also clutched the earth with twisted roots. These resembled tentacles smeared with dirt and caressed by faceless worms. Logically, larger flower heads kept balance with bigger and danker roots hidden underground. The flowers also fed bees.

5. Challenge me all who remain. Anyone?

6. Throughout it everybody regularly ate food, consumed liquid, and used the washroom (contrary to popular belief). They dined out of sight. Men touched up their appearances in bathroom mirrors behind closed doors and elegantly beautiful women experienced a rumbling, groaning agony.

7. There were always tears in secret when laughter rang out in public.

8. It's over. Write anything here but it's still over. Nothing but memories although they play like dreams. Add new people? No. Now isn't the time or place. We can still discuss those who've gone, but here and now? They'd only be me twisted into different forms, only me here all alone where there's nothing left to come and only endless sorting out of the past left. Why? Who are they to make it all so convoluted, secretive, and contradictory that the last one left here can't just accept the infinite emptiness following the end? Why do they have to endure the torture of revisiting the past to sort out all the careless mistakes woven into it?

9. At first we saw it as amusing. Then it grew boring. Finally it became unbearable torment. It was decided that the whole thing (or the lack of it) just needed to be over. So it ended "quietly and "without ceremony." Although now I wish there had been a ceremony to see it all off. Memory is all there is now and it might be interesting or entertaining at least if there had been a celebration. All that endures is instead a reflection filled with disinterest and lost spirit. When the time

for celebration approached as the thing ended there was no energy to plan anything, but there was a reason. Now that the time for celebration has passed there's plenty of energy to plan something, but there's no reason to do so. Yet, as the last one left, the sole keeper of the records and modifications in these addenda, no one remains to challenge me. So let's say this (who is there to say otherwise?): we had a celebration, a legendary one. Fireworks exploded so bright and varied their flowers grew and overtook the sky. Untold legions of royal guards blew silver trumpets. In every one of the earth's corners wizards of ecstasy entranced the millions with lasers dancing overhead. And they all danced in a singular, self-contained night that lasted forever because it had absolutely zero awareness of dawn.

10. Yes. That's it. The corrections are made, the illusions are lifted, and the ending may be remembered with sweet nostalgia and pride. I can stop speaking. Now it's truly finished.

END

Select Spoken Word Performances

-Poetry Reading during Former Mayor Hazel McCallion's 99th Birthday at the Vic Johnson C.C. in Streetsville

--February 14th 2020

-Robbie Burns Day Tea at the Benares Historic House

--January 26th 2020

-Poetry Reading during Councillor Chris Fonseca's Family Fun Skate at the Burnhamthorpe C.C. Indoor Arena

--January 24th 2020

-Mississauga Mayor Bonnie Crombie's 2020 New Year's Levee in City Council Chambers.

--January 12th 2020

-Featured Set at Best of Open Mic at MAKE in Make Café and Catering in Milton

--November 30th 2019

-Host, Organizer, and Poet at the Outer Haven Poetry Series at Little London Café in Brampton

--November 25th 2019, with a second edition
occurring on January 17th 2019

-In Flanders Fields Recitation at the City of Mississauga's Remembrance Day Ceremony outside the Civic Centre

--November 11th 2019

-Featured Poet at the Shab-e She'r Poetry Series in Toronto in the Tranzac Club

--October 30th 2019

-Featured Poet at the Oakville Literary Café in the Joshua Creek Heritage Arts Centre

--October 20th 2019

-Featured Poet at the Art Bar Poetry Series in the Free Times Café

--August 13th 2019

-Featured Poet at the 1st Annual Arts at the Port Festival by the Port Credit BIA in St. Lawrence Square

--Sunday, July 21st 2019

-Canada Day Reading at Celebration Square in Mississauga for the City's Canada Celebration

--July 1st 2019

-Featured Poet at the Open Mic at MAKE in Make Café and Catering, Milton

--May 24th 2019

-Co-host, Co-Organizer, and Poet at the Verses Out Loud Poetry Series at the Common Ground Café in Mississauga, in association with the Mississauga Arts Council

-April 4th 2019 and continuing for six more editions until November 2019

-Poetry Reading during the inauguration ceremony for becoming the 3rd Mississauga Poet Laureate at Mississauga City Hall in the Council Chambers.

-April 3rd 2019

-Featured Poet at the Oakville Poetry and Prose Open Mic held by Sheila Tucker in Taste of Colombia Fair Trade Coffee

--December 1th 2018

-Featured Poet at the More Songs and Poems Series hosted by Max Layton at Tranzac Club in Toronto

--November 11th 2018

-Featured Poet at Wild Writers Poetry Salon in Poetry Jazz Café, Toronto

--October 2nd 2018

-Host and Poet for Paul's Poetry Night #13 at Full of Beans Coffee House and Roastery in Toronto

--June 22nd 2018

-Poet and MC for the After the Freeze Art Showcase by the Peel Arts Collective at Spot 1 Grill and Music Hall in Brampton

--May 19th 2018

-Featured Poet at Norman Cristofoli's Literature and Music Salon in Toronto

--January 13th 2018

-Poetry Reading at the Brampton Book Bash by the Festival of Literary Diversity in Brampton City Hall

--September 30th 2017

-Host and Poet for the YTGA Open Mic Series at Studio.89 in Mississauga

--July 30th 2017 and continuing through
to the present on a monthly basis.

Select Publications

PRINT indicates a publication mainly available in a physical print copy

A URL indicates that the publication was in an online periodical

POETRY COLLECTION

"THE LONG TRAIN OF CHAOS"
Kung Fu Treachery Press. (Fall 2019).
Available in person and at Barnes and Noble.

POETRY

"The King will Hide and the People will be Afraid"
The Flying Walrus Vol. 42, Issue #1 (September 2010). Print.

Six Poems
The Eunoia Review (March 2015). https://bit.ly/2Gp256r

"Demon's Whisper: Morningstar"
Songs of Eretz Poetry Review (July 2015). https://bit.ly/2Naqjlq

"Once the Strings are Cut, All Fall Down"
REAL: Regarding Arts and Letters (June 2016). Print and Online.
https://issuu.com/reallitmag/docs/real_39_2/1

"I Met my Childhood Hero and he Wants to Kill Me" dryland_lit press (Winter 2017). Print.

"Magic Lamp Semantics"
Gyroscope Review (June 2018).
https://bit.ly/2E9OCwG

"The Last Landlines to the Source"
Brick Books (July 2018)-*Paid publication*
https://bit.ly/2GIRFxE –AUDIO RECORDING

"Elixir of Ordnance"
PØST-: poésie contemporaine/contemporary poetry
(March 2019).
https://revuepost.com/elixir-of-ordnance/

"Set the Truth on Our Ground"
Modern Mississauga Media. (Summer 2019).
https://issuu.com/modernmississauga/docs/mm21_latesummer19-r2

Three Poems
Former People Journal (Fall 2019)
https://formerpeople.wordpress.com/2019/11/30/three-poems-67/

"Speak Friend and Enter"
Auroras and Blossoms Poetry Journal. (Spring 2020).
https://abpoetryjournal.com/

"Where No Suns Shine"
Pif Magazine (April 2020)-
https://t.co/LvT7tB5zpo?amp=1
*Also published in video format on the Mississauga Culture Facebook Page.
https://www.facebook.com/saugaculture/videos/533289414023838/

Three Poems
Unlikely Stories Mark V (April 2020).
https://www.unlikelystories.org/content/madman-above-the-city-my-mind-stripped-bare-by-its-absence-uneven-and-criminological

"Fist of the Third-Quarter Moon"
Malfunction Literary Magazine (May 2020)
https://www.malfunctionlitmag.com/paul-edward-costa-fist-of-the-third

Four Poems
Otherwise Engaged Literature and Arts Journal (End of May 2020).

Three Poems
The Misfit Quill (Summer 2020).
https://5e6eab5bab330.site123.me/

The Daughter of Oceanus
Flora Fiction Literary Magazine (Summer 2020)

SHORT STORIES

"Green Martyrdom"
Thrice Fiction #11 (August 2014).
http://www.thricefiction.com/archives.html

"The Quiet Sentinel"
The J.J. Outre Review Issue #2 (April 2015). https://bit.ly/2SM-5TEw

"Transference"
Crack the Spine Literary Magazine (October 2016).
http://www.crackthespine.com/

"Archangel IX"
Rainfall Books: Space Adventures #4 (February 2017). Print.

"Distorted Reflections of a Pilgrim"
Queen Mob's Teahouse Literary Journal (May 2017).
https://bit.ly/2N5ls4Q

"Princess Senux and the Half-Sun Leviathan"
Mannequin Haus: A Journal of Literary Art (September 2017).
https://bit.ly/2GIxVdF

"Our Broadcasting Day"
Enduring Puberty Press (Autumn 2017).
https://miuseofheterolinea.wordpress.com/

"The Transmutation of Embers"
Aphelion: The Webzine of Science Fiction and Fantasy (December 2017).
https://bit.ly/2UTtNuY

"Priests of the Khravik"
Bewildering Stories (Spring 2019).

"Rainbows and Black Tumours"
Lucent Dream Issue #4 (Summer 2019).

FLASH FICTION

"The Chronicle of Everything"
Timber Journal (October 2013). Print. http://www.timberjournal.com/?p=235

"The Zero Second"
Yesteryear Fiction (September 2014).
https://bit.ly/2SP6NzV

"A Sailboat on the Radio Waves"
Emerge Literary Journal Issue #9 (December 2014). Print.

"Patience and Disassociation"
The Bookends Review (January 2016).
http://bit.ly/2nn4d1M

"Tales of Telyhurst Castle: Reverend Arturo's Flock"
Sein Und Werden (June 2016).
https://bit.ly/2Bx0U0n

"The Vanity of the Necromancer"
Bonk! Magazine (Autumn 2016). Print.

"The Lone and Level Sands will Stretch Far Away" (with author's statement on "beauty")
Peacock Journal (June 2017). https://bit.ly/2Gqm4Bs

"The Lucid Dream of an Analog Clock" (with author's statement on "beauty")
Peacock Journal (December 2017).
https://bit.ly/2E9teb8

"The Forest Sprite Cannot Hear the Whispering Trees"
Tiny Flames Press (Summer 2018).
https://bit.ly/2BBDCXz

"The Modern Theseus"
Synaeresis: Arts + Poetry Issue #10 (Spring 2020).

NON-FICTION

"Give me your Hand, it's Dark and I Know the Way"
-Review of "Finger:Knuckle:Palm" by Ariana Den Bleyker Entropy
(August 2014).http://bit.ly/2nmRUCi

INTERVIEWS

Interview with Paul Edward Costa by Valentino Assenza at the University of Toronto for the CIUT 89.5 FM "Howl" Radio Show. Recorded on May 29th 2018.

Interview with Paul Edward Costa by The Mississauga Arts Council for its M.A.C. Member Series-Video
November 2018.
https://bit.ly/2FBCFj1

Interview with Paul Edward Costa by Jay Kana
of Modern Mississauga Magazine
April 2019.
https://issuu.com/modernmississauga/docs/mm19_spring19-r4